In the Shadow of Goll

by Tony Abbott
Illustrated by David Merrell
Cover illustration by Tim Jessell

A
LITTLE APPLE
PAPERBACK

SCHOLASTIC INC.
New York Toronto London Auckland Sydney
Mexico City New Delhi Hong Kong Buenos Aires

To Amanda
with love always

For more information about the continuing saga of Droon,
please visit Tony Abbott's website at
www.tonyabbottbooks.com

ISBN 0-439-67176-0

Text copyright © 2006 by Tony Abbott.
Illustrations copyright © 2006 by Scholastic Inc.

12 11 10 9 8 7 6 5 4 3   6 7 8 9 10 11/0

Printed in the U.S.A.   40
First printing, July 2006

Contents

One

The Magic of Friends

Eric Hinkle stood under the rafters of his dusty attic and read aloud from a large golden scroll.

"Okay. Sit on the floor, cross your legs, close your eyes, touch your knee, tap your nose, and nod your head."

With a giant blue turban pressed low over his brow, Eric's friend Neal Kroger plopped down on the floor and began tapping and nodding. "You mean like this?" he asked.

Eric glanced at him, then back at the scroll. "That seems right. Now say, '*Tembo-lembo-polly-molly-zoot-boot!*'"

Continuing to tap and nod, Neal drew in a long breath and said the words.

All of a sudden — *fwoosh!* — he floated straight up to the ceiling, nearly grazing his head on the rafters.

"Awesome!" he cried.

"Now it says to lean forward," said Eric. Neal did. *Whooom!* He shot across the attic, narrowly missing Eric's head. Leaning to one side and then the other, he zigzagged back between towers of cartons and storage boxes.

"This is amazing!" said Neal. "It's stupendous! It's terrific! It's —"

"Magic?" said Eric.

"You got that right!" Neal slowed, tilted

his head, and began spinning over the attic stairs.

Eric laughed. It *was* magic. It was genie magic, and Neal had gotten it from the mysterious land of Droon.

Droon was the magical world Eric, Neal, and their friend Julie had discovered one day under his basement stairs. It was a place of enchantment and adventure, a land of close friends and powerful enemies.

It was there that they had met the young wizard Princess Keeah, her teacher, the great wizard Galen, and their spider troll friend, Max. It was there that they had battled sorcerers and beasts of every kind imaginable.

Droon was where Julie had been scratched by a creature called a wingwolf and had developed the ability to fly and to change shape.

Because of Droon, Eric was discovering

that he himself had the powers of a major wizard.

And finally, Droon was where Neal was revealed to be none other than the magical, time-traveling First Genie of the Dove!

"Wait until Julie sees me do my stuff!" said Neal, zipping by Eric again and snatching the scroll from his hand. "Man, I really love this!"

Laughing, Eric realized he loved it, too. Having powers didn't only mean that Neal could use ancient genie magic to help battle the bad guys. It also meant that since each of the three friends now possessed special powers, it wasn't even about magic anymore.

It was what it was supposed to be about — being plain old friends.

Neal paused over Eric's head, chuckled to himself, then whispered some words from the scroll. *Pooof!* A small steaming pie appeared in the air in front of him.

"That was fast!" said Eric with a smile.

Neal took a bite of the pie and grinned. "I think this genie thing is going to be good."

But just when Neal was about to conjure a glass of milk — *stomp! stomp!* — someone opened the attic door and started up the stairs.

"Holy cow!" gasped Eric. "It's my dad —"

Neal flailed suddenly, then dropped to the floor in a heap. Both boys turned to the stairs to see a tall man wearing a flannel shirt and paint-stained pants, staring at them over his glasses.

"Uh, hi, Dad!" said Eric nervously.

"Ditto, Mr. H!" added Neal. "I mean, not the 'Dad' part, but the 'hi' part —"

"Neal," said Mr. Hinkle. "I saw you flying! You must be a . . . a . . . *genie!*"

Neal gasped. He and Eric looked at each other with wide eyes. "But . . . how did you know?"

A long moment of silence was followed by a bright laugh. Then Mr. Hinkle started to wobble and shrink and blur. A few seconds later — *floop!* — it wasn't Eric's father standing there anymore. It was their friend Julie.

"Julie!" said Neal. "You scared us to death! I thought our secret was out. Nobody's supposed to know about Droon."

"Sorry!" she said, laughing. "I couldn't resist! I don't get many chances to use my shape-shifting powers —"

Boing — boing — boing — thunk!

"Eric!" called a deep voice from downstairs. "What did I tell you about playing soccer in the house? Do I have to come up there?"

The three friends stared at one another.

"It wasn't me this time!" Julie whispered.

Boing — thonk — boing — boing!

"What's going on?" said Eric. He looked down just in time to see a soccer ball bounce across the floor below. It rolled to a stop at the foot of the attic stairs.

"What is *that* doing *here*?" asked Neal.

The kids' soccer ball had been charmed long ago by Princess Keeah. When she wanted her friends to join her in Droon, she often used the ball to send a coded message. But the kids always kept the ball in Eric's basement.

Boing! The soccer ball bounced up onto the bottom step.

"Eric!" Mrs. Hinkle called.

"Sorry!" In a flash, Eric ran down the stairs, scooped up the ball, and carried it up to the attic. As he did, words began to appear on its surface.

Roov-Harga

The kids knew the letters were in reverse.

"Agrah-Voor," said Julie. "The city of ghosts. Sparr told us to go there the last time we were in Droon."

Right, thought Eric. *Sparr.*

Droon was about *him*, too.

The first time the three friends had ever met Sparr, he was a superpowerful, black-cloaked, fish-finned evil sorcerer. Not long ago, however, Sparr had fallen victim to his own magic and been transformed back into a boy.

As a boy, Sparr had been helping the kids. He had even become their friend.

Right now, Sparr was with the wicked beast ruler, Emperor Ko, and his second-in-command, Gethwing, secretly hoping to defeat them. He had sent a secret message to the kids that the emperor's armies were gathering for battle in the terrible Serpent Sea. He'd also told them that something bad was happening in nearby Agrah-Voor.

Eric hoped their friend wasn't in danger, but as hard as he tried to think otherwise, he knew it was only a hope.

Sparr was in the very heart of evil now.

"Keeah, Galen, and Max are probably already in Agrah-Voor," said Neal, folding his magic turban and rolling up his scroll to the tiniest size imaginable. Then he stuffed them both into his pocket. "If they need reinforcements, that means us, and that means now."

In a few quick moments, the three of them had run down the attic stairs, down the main stairs, through the kitchen, and into the basement. Eric placed the soccer ball — which was normal once more — on the workbench. Then he turned to the little storage closet under the basement stairs and smiled.

"It's Droon time again!" he said.

The three friends turned on the closet light, piled in, and closed the door behind them.

"Let me," said Julie. She reached for the ceiling light and pulled its short chain.

Click. The light went out. The closet was pitch-black for a moment. Then it wasn't.

Whoosh! In a blaze of color, the floor became the top step of a long, curving staircase. As always, Eric's heart beat faster when he saw the magic stairs appear.

The fabulous world of Droon — and a new adventure — were waiting for them.

They started quickly down the rainbow-colored stairs, curving into the sky below. But no sooner had they climbed down through Droon's wispy pink clouds than the air grew thick and dark around them. It began to feel close, as if they were inside. By the time the kids climbed down the last few steps, the space surrounding them was as black as night.

Stepping onto solid earth, Eric paused and sniffed in every direction. "It smells wet."

Neal slipped his turban on his head and moved forward in the dark. "I sense a stream of water very close. It's five, no, six inches deep."

Julie peered over his shoulder. "Your genie powers can tell you how deep the water is?"

"No, but my genie feet can," said Neal, looking down. "I just stepped in it up to my ankles."

Sure enough, they could just make out the glinting surface of a narrow stream. It wove down a tunnel ahead of them. Bobbing next to the bank not far away was a small wooden boat.

Julie gasped. "We've been in that boat before, guys. It sails to Agrah-Voor —"

"Shhh!" Eric turned his head. In the distance, he heard an eerie humming sound. It echoed against the walls of the tunnel.

Then something moved in the dark.

Before anyone could speak, the tall, shadowy figure of a man appeared in the passage, dragging a dark sack on the ground behind him. The man wore a ragged black cloak from head to foot. A deep hood covered nearly his whole face, except for a pair of burning red eyes staring from beneath its quivering folds.

Purple mist swirled all around him. It coiled about his cloak tails and fluttered around the frayed ends of his hood like smoke stirred by heat.

He saw the children and kept coming.

Tensing, Eric pointed his fingers at the man. They sparked with silver light. "Stop where you are," he said. "I'm a wizard —"

"And I'm Zabilac, the genie!" said Neal, frantically searching his scroll for a charm. "And I'm a really fast reader —"

The man stopped and raised his hand toward the children. His fingers were thin and pale. In a faltering whisper, as if struggling to get even the smallest sound out, he spoke.

"Ny . . . Ny . . . Nyora!"

Then, in a breath, with no more than a tiny movement of the air, he was gone.

"But . . . where did he *go*?" asked Eric.

"Never mind — that sounded like a spell!" said Julie. "Brace yourselves!"

Ten seconds went by. Twenty seconds.

The boat bobbed in the stream. The black water lapped quietly against the banks.

When two minutes had passed, Eric turned to his friends. "So maybe 'Nyora' wasn't a spell after all?"

Neal snorted. "I guess seeing the official First Genie of the Dove scared him. Even though I sort of lied about being a fast reader. He and his stinky purple cloud are long gone."

But Julie had already started toward the boat. "Guys, I smell something else — smoke. What if it's coming from Agrah-Voor? What if Agrah-Voor is on fire?"

"We should get down there!" said Eric.

Without another word, the three friends raced down the bank and jumped into the boat. As it had done the first time they rode in it, the boat mysteriously pulled away from the bank and sailed swiftly down the river to the ghost city of Agrah-Voor.

Two

Name the Bad Guy

Remembering what he did once before in the boat, Eric dipped his hand into the stream. At once, the dark water turned crystal clear.

"There it is!" said Neal, pointing down through the water. "The land of ghosts. Where the dead people live."

The great walled city of Agrah-Voor was an imposing mass of stone on the gray plains below the water. Many centuries old and many miles across, it was a place of towers and bridges, palaces and fountains. As the children looked now, they saw a plume of smoke twisting up from its far wall.

"I was right," said Julie. "It *is* on fire —"

"Hold on tight!" said Eric. "Going down!"

Just as it had the first time they went to Agrah-Voor, the little boat began to dip.

Silvery waves rushed over the boat's bow, completely drenching the children. Then, a moment later, they were completely dry again and floating through the air *underneath* the river.

The closer they got to the city, the better they could see that the tall column of smoke was tinged with purple mist.

"I guess we know who started the fire," said Julie. "That creepy shadow guy."

"I think I'll call him Shadowface," said

Neal. "Because we couldn't see his face. A creepy name for a creepy guy."

The boat drifted inside the city walls, then thudded down amid a group of ghostly soldiers trying to douse the flames. Among them, Eric caught sight of Princess Keeah and her parents, King Zello and Queen Relna.

"Eric! Julie! Neal!" Keeah called, running to them. "This fire is magical. The more we try to put it out, the more it grows!"

"So Shadowhood *can* do magic," said Julie.

"Shadowface," said Neal. "I call him —"

"Stand back!" boomed a great, deep voice. There was a sudden rush of wind, and the wizard Galen swept in among them, icicles dripping from his long blue cloak. Right behind him were his little friend Max, whose orange hair was covered with giant snowflakes, and Kem, Sparr's two-headed pet dog.

"Hello, children!" chirped Max. "We've just come from the far north. The *very* far north!"

"Purple fire needs the purple water of Tembish-Pa!" Galen shouted. Then he murmured a mystical charm and swung a large frosty bucket out from his cloak.

A splash of purple water rolled through the air and grew and grew until it was as tall as a wave. It crashed against the fiery wall with a great *hissss!* and the flames went out.

"Hooray!" yelled the warriors. "Three cheers for the wizard Galen —"

"Wait!" said a voice behind the crowd, and the warriors went silent. They parted and bowed as an old woman wearing a strange crown of antlers came forward.

It was Queen Hazad, the longtime ruler of Agrah-Voor. Her crown glinted in the dying embers. As the smoke cleared, she sighed heavily.

"Oh, no . . . it's as I feared. No, no, no."

"Hazad?" said Zello. "What is it —"

Then everyone saw what the queen was staring at. In a hole in the wall stood an iron chest. Its lid had toppled to one side, and the chest was empty. Kem approached it cautiously, sniffing.

Eric trembled. "What was in there?"

Hazad turned to him. "The Warriors of the Skorth were buried there. They're gone!"

The Warriors of the Skorth were magical skeletons brought to life long ago by Sparr at his evil worst. After being destroyed at Agrah-Voor by Galen and the children, their loose bones were entombed in the city wall.

Max grumbled as he waved away the

remaining purple smoke. "Those nasty bone men are back? Who would steal them?"

"Other than Sparr himself," said Relna, "who could possibly bring them back to life?"

Eric glanced at Julie and Neal. "Uh . . ."

"Children?" said Galen. "You look as if you've seen a ghost, except that the ghosts here are not so frightening, I think!"

Eric couldn't get the image of the hooded man out of his mind. "We saw someone."

"Who was it?" asked Keeah.

"No one we've ever seen before," said Julie.

"We didn't actually see him this time, either," added Neal. "He's seven feet tall and as thin as a stick. His face was hidden under a huge hood. I call him . . . Shadowface."

Kem grumbled at the sound of the name.

"Did he fight you?" asked Max.

Eric shook his head. "All he did was say a single word. I had never heard it before. 'Nyora.'"

"We thought he was putting a curse on us, but nothing happened," said Julie.

"Nyora," repeated Queen Hazad. "Perhaps it is a curse. But whatever language it is, it's not one I've heard before."

"Shadowman, eh?" Max snarled. "So now we have a new villain in Droon —"

"Shadowface," said Neal. "I think we've all agreed to call him Shadowface."

Keeah frowned. "What if he's part of Emperor Ko's plan?" she asked. "I mean, Sparr already warned us that Ko's armies were gathering in the Serpent Sea. We're pretty close to the Serpent Sea here. Maybe Shadowcloak is on his way there."

"Shadow*face*," said Neal, frowning.

"When one evil rises," said Galen, "it

brings another evil with it, and another and another. Emperor Ko. Gethwing, the moon dragon. It was only a matter of time before a new evil arose."

Neal dug into his pocket and pulled out his scroll. "But don't forget, we have a new good guy now, too. Even if I can't use all my powers yet."

Galen grinned. "You will be handy today, no doubt. But some of us have known for a long time that the greatness of Neal Kroger has little to do with magic!"

Neal blushed.

King Zello nodded firmly. "I will return to Jaffa City at once and bring the Droon navy back with me. Ko's beast army must not be allowed out of the Serpent Sea. Max, will you pilot the *Jaffa Wind* and lead our fleet?"

The spider troll grinned from ear to ear.

"At your service, my king. With me at the helm, we'll be back in no time!"

"And no time is what we have," said Relna. "Queen Hazad, there's no greater library for lost languages than Agrah-Voor's library of the dead. Working together, you and I may discover what 'Nyora' means. And perhaps who this Shadoweyes is."

Neal opened his mouth, then closed it again without saying anything.

"Let's all meet at the Horns of Ko before the first stroke of battle," said Galen.

"Better yet," said Eric, "let's hope that battle never happens."

"Good words!" chirped Max. "Let's go!"

"One more thing," said Galen. He looked over at Keeah. Around her neck hung the silver Moon Medallion, an object of great power created by Galen's mother, Queen Zara. "This may be in danger today, my dear. Let your father hide it in Jaffa City under lock and key. For safety."

"Of course," Keeah said. She lifted the Medallion over her head and handed it to the king.

Zello then embraced his wife and daughter and raced away with Max to the city gates.

"We must steal away, too —" said Galen.

"Did someone say *steal*?" piped up a voice.

Everyone turned as — *fwish!* — a creature with a long snout and wispy whiskers appeared before them, twining a rope over his shoulder. He was dressed entirely in silky green, from his fancy vest to his curly-toed slippers.

"Shago!" cried Keeah. "We could use your help today!"

"That's why I came," said the rat-whiskered master thief and longtime resident of Agrah-Voor. "A thief steals everything, including what people say. I heard every word you said. I know the Skorth were stolen. I know you must find this Shadowfog character —"

"Face," said Neal grimly.

"Quite right," said Shago. "Fogface. But time is wasting. Hurry. Walk this way!"

He dropped on all fours and scuttled sideways across the main square of Agrah-Voor to its central fountain, his snout pressed close to the ground.

Galen made a face at the children. "I don't think Shago means that we actually have to walk that way. . . ."

"I hope not!" said Keeah.

"Ah, ah, yes!" called the whiskered thief. "Already I smell the trail. Hurry! Follow the dead skeletons!"

Eric sighed. "That's pretty much my favorite thing to do!"

As quickly as they had come, the friends left Agrah-Voor through the city's enormous Gate of Life, with Sparr's pet, Kem, trotting quickly after them. Once outside, they headed for a pool of dark, moving water. Without a pause, they jumped in and soon found themselves back on the surface of Droon, as dry as before.

Moments later, the little band was speeding away from the city of fallen heroes and heading into the dreaded Dark Lands toward the Serpent Sea.

Three

At the Horns of Ko

"Let's be on our guard," said Keeah. "Who knows why Shadowface stole the Skorth, or what he's really up to?"

"For the last time, his name is Shadowhood!" yelled Neal. Then he crinkled his face up in confusion. "Wait. No. Sorry. Shadowface. Shadowface is right!"

"Or, rather, Shadowface is left!" said Shago, pointing. "That way, over the plains to the eastern foothills. His trail is slow but steady. Come!"

Taking the lead, Shago raced across the plains. The rises and dips in the land were followed by a long, slow incline toward a range of jagged mountains.

One hour, two hours, they traveled. Finally, at midday they approached the summit of the black mountains.

"Ho, ho, ho, and what have we here?" Shago said, raising his hand for them to stop.

"Do you see something?" asked Eric.

Bending close to a thorny hedge that snaked along the mountaintops, Shago sniffed a tiny leaf that dangled from a branch. He plucked the leaf, crinkled it, licked it, and finally popped it into his mouth.

"This leaf," he proclaimed, "is very good for sauces!"

Keeah frowned. "Now, Shago —"

"It's also good for another reason," said the thief, tugging on his whiskers. "Its fragrance fills the air when it has been broken. This particular leaf was broken by someone walking by it. Very recently, too. Kem, bring your snouts. Let us look further!"

As Shago and the dog scampered along the ridge, Galen began to pace back and forth, his staff shimmering with light.

"I have a feeling that the things put into motion today will not end well," he said. He paused and pulled a small object from his cloak. It was a lump of black stone.

The children had seen it before. Galen had recently gone on a long journey. It was on that journey that he discovered the stone.

"Everyone, listen here," he said. "The time has come to tell you what I know about this object and why I wanted the Moon Medallion far away from us today."

Holding the small stone in his hand, Galen explained, "This little lump is one of three my mother, Queen Zara, charmed long ago. She wanted to give one to each of her three sons: Sparr, Urik, and me."

Keeah looked as if she wanted to ask a question, but the wizard went on.

"Together, the three stones form pieces of my mother's powerful Moon Medallion. You know two of the stones already. From the one I was given, I fashioned the Ring of Midnight. It fits around the Medallion and helps reveal some of my mother's long-hidden secrets and powers. When Urik's stone was given to him, he created nothing less than the Pearl Sea —"

Eric nearly choked. "Wait. What? *Urik* made the Pearl Sea? But I found the Pearl

Sea in my mother's closet! How did it get into my house?"

"Eric!" said Galen sharply. "That is a question for another day. For now — for right now — let me finish. My mother died before giving Sparr his stone. This stone. Because it appeared worthless, it was lost. And because it was lost, it has remained all these years an unformed lump."

The wizard breathed a deep, long sigh.

"I tell you this because . . . because I feel that today we are entering a time in which the forces of evil are changing shape in Droon. A new villain is upon us. My brother Sparr is in grave danger. The battle — the war! — between freedom and tyranny is upon us. This stone, this shapeless little lump, may hold the key to Droon's future. Unlocking the true power of the Moon Medallion may be the only thing —"

"Galen, everyone!" Shago said suddenly

as he rushed down from the very top of the ridge. "Look what Kem and I have found!"

Everyone ran with him to where the dog stood, both its heads pointing over the ridge into a deep valley of scorched sand. They hid behind the ridge and carefully peeked over.

"Whoa, look!" said Neal. "It's him . . . himself!"

In a semicircle of rocks at the center of the valley stood the hooded figure, looming over a pile of bones. A ragged sack lay empty nearby. As the figure waved his arms, hisses and murmurings drifted up the sides of the valley.

Then the bones began to move — *click-clack!*

"Holy cow!" whispered Julie. "It's just like Sparr did so long ago. Shadowface knows how to bring the skeletons back to life!"

Eric wanted everything to stop so he could think about how he had found the magical Pearl Sea in his mother's closet. He wanted to remember once more the milky-white stone and feel its strange beauty and power.

But nothing stopped. As he watched the clattering bones begin to assemble themselves, Eric thought instead about Sparr.

The boy had given them countless clues about what Emperor Ko and the moon dragon Gethwing were doing. But was Sparr safe? How long would Ko and Gethwing trust him? Sparr knew that the moon dragon wanted to overthrow the emperor. When would that happen? And how was Shadowface involved in all of it? What, if anything, did Sparr know about *him*? What was really going on?

Floing! A skull rose in the air and

hovered there. Next a neck and ribs clattered out of the bone pile and gathered under it. Two arms flew up and attached themselves to shoulders. First one leg then the other wobbled from the ground and connected to the other bones.

At last, the skeleton warrior bowed to Shadowface. When it stood upright once more, it wore a helmet on its head and held a short, curved sword by its side.

"Not only dead but magically armored, too," said Keeah. "Is that creepy or what?"

"Creepy," murmured Julie. "Definitely."

Before long, nine Skorth warriors stood at attention before the hooded figure.

With a yell that sounded almost like a wail of pain, Shadowface led the warriors across the valley floor and toward the Serpent Sea.

Galen made a noise under his breath. "The Skorth may be fierce warriors, perhaps

even unstoppable, but there are only nine of them. Neal," he said, a little smile on his lips, "what do you think of using your powers of time travel, my genie friend?"

Neal grinned. "Really? Can I?"

"Go as far back as you can to discover why anyone would want the Skorth," said the wizard. "Find out if they have a secret. Take Kem with you, if you like. Then meet us at the Horns of Ko. We'll go there now."

As their friends left, Neal and the dog plopped on the ground. The boy crossed his legs, read from his scroll, and — *ploomf!* — both he and Kem vanished from sight.

Three hours later, the little band arrived at the border of the Dark Lands. As usual, the sky was smoky, black, and foul.

Standing as sentinels between free

Droon and the Dark Lands were two huge floating rocks, each carved in the shape of Ko's bull-like head. Known as the Horns of Ko, each massive rock bore three enormous eyes of red stone, the twin horns of a bull, and long tusks as sharp as sword blades. They faced each other on either side of a narrow channel. There, the crystal water of the Sea of Droon met the sluggish black waves of the Serpent Sea.

"The Empire of Goll began here," said Shago nervously. "Do you think —"

"I do think!" said Galen. "Ko wants to bring that empire back. Gethwing wants to bring it back. Perhaps this Shadowface wants to bring it back, too. It's our job to see that they don't!"

Together, the friends climbed up the rocks and found themselves atop the northernmost side of the twin Horns of Ko.

Looking down, they saw Shadowface

lead the Skorth warriors behind the Horns. The ten figures were welcomed there by the largest army of beasts the kids could imagine.

As far as the eye could see, both banks of the channel were covered with thousands and thousands of beasts — furred, scaled, winged, and finned.

"The army of armies!" Galen muttered gloomily. "It looks like Ko does plan to start his great war today."

Eric gazed down the channel. "I remember this place. So does my stomach. I feel sick —"

"You should have said something. I would have brought more pie," said a familiar voice.

Everyone turned, and there were Neal and Kem, waving away a puff of smoke. Neal had a patch over one eye and wore a pair of huge boots. Kem's heads were wrapped with bright red bandannas.

"Nice outfits," said Shago. "Where have you been?"

Neal removed the eye patch. "Actually, right here. It was about ten thousand years ago, and these two big rocks didn't have Ko's creepy face on them yet."

"Before the beginnings of Goll itself!" mused Galen. "What did you find out?"

"Lots," said Neal. "For instance, did you know that the Skorth were originally pirates? Well, they were. And right here in this channel is where their fleet of pirate ships was sunk in one of Droon's first-ever sea battles!"

Galen made a low gasp. "So *that* is why we're here! Shadowface has brought the Skorth here to raise their ancient ships. They will become Ko's navy!"

"Here's the other thing," said Neal, pulling off his boots and revealing his sneakers underneath. "The legend goes that once the Skorth ships are raised, no earthly vessel can sink them —"

Before they could move, they heard a sudden shout from below. Peering down, they saw the Skorth warriors dive one by one into the black water, cheered on by the beasts. In nearly no time, giant bubbles burst on the surface, and one after another, a fleet of ghostly ships began to rise from the depths.

"Those ships are huge!" exclaimed Julie.

"And scary!" added Keeah.

"Rooo!" agreed Kem.

What they first saw bursting up from the water were the huge black skulls carved on the prow of each boat. Their jaws were gaping wide in toothless grins.

Next came the vessels' rotten sails, hanging in shreds from broken masts. Garlands of seaweed and black vines clung to the remains of the rigging and the shattered decks. Finally, as water rushed off the sides, ugly holes appeared, gaping among the hull planks and showing the wooden "bones" beneath the ships' ghostly skin.

And yet, as unseaworthy as each ship seemed to be, they all rose with a great crash of water and bobbed heavily on the surface.

The beasts on the shore cheered over and over as each new vessel appeared in the channel.

"I don't see Shadowface," said Keeah, scanning the shore. "He must be hiding."

"But look there," said Shago suddenly. "It's young Sparr himself, flying in on the dragon's back. Hide!"

Together, everyone dashed under an

outcropping of rock. Peering up, they saw the spiky wings of Gethwing soaring over the channel. On his back sat young Sparr, his black cloak flying up behind him, his pale little face looking toward the ground. When the dragon landed on a wide ledge below, Sparr slid off his back and followed him into an opening in one of the stone heads.

"If there will be a battle," said Eric, "then Sparr's in danger. He's trapped right in the middle of it now. If only we could sneak down there and get him out . . ."

"I can change into a beast," said Julie. "And maybe even get past the guards. But I don't think I can do it alone —"

"Whoa, that reminds me!" said Neal. "I was skimming my favorite scroll and found a genie thing called a triple charm. You can take one person's ability and share it with three other people. Julie, if you disguise yourself as a beast, we can, too."

The children looked at one another.

"Teamwork," said Galen, smiling. "It's what we're all about, isn't it? And I've just had another thought. If no earthly ship can sink the Skorth vessels, perhaps they can sink one another. I'll steal down to the shore —"

"There's that word *steal* again!" said Shago, piping up. "Stealing is a job for a thief. Besides, I rather like my shape, curling whiskers and all. So if the wizard will have me, I'll go with him."

"Kem should go with you, too," said Neal. "He'll probably be safer."

Galen chuckled as he started down the stone head. "And what an excellent team we shall make! Friends, stay safe. Neal, read that charm carefully!"

Neal grinned. "Hey, I got a C-plus on my last reading test. So we'll be okay —"

"Uh, Neal," said Julie, "maybe I should —"

Without pausing, Neal waved his hands and began mumbling the triple charm, *"Wolly-golly-pumbo-jumbo . . ."*

In a twinkling, he and his friends began to change into four very large, very strange, very shaggy beasts.

Four

Meet the Blugs

Thump-squish-thump!

Pacing the narrow ledge, Eric found himself completely covered in shaggy gray fur from his big head to his tiny feet. His *three* tiny feet, one of which made gooey prints on the ground.

Neal laughed at Eric. "Nice look!" But he stopped laughing when he saw that he had three feet, too. "Oh, man! What *are* we?"

Julie parted the fur in front of her face and peered out with a pair of tiny red eyes. "Hey, I'm really sorry, guys, but beasts are beasts."

"Never mind," said Keeah. "Let's get Sparr out of there, and us out of here. Come on."

Although climbing with three feet was not easy, the four friends made their way as quickly as possible down the stone head until they arrived at the opening where Gethwing and Sparr had entered. Two beasts stood guard outside the chamber. Each had a face like a potato that tapered to a point, and a thick tuft of hair that fell down over both ears like a fountain.

"Is mighty Gethwing expecting you?" demanded one of the guards.

"Yeah, well, not exactly," said Eric, surprised to find his voice high and whiny.

"Then you are spies!" said the other.

"No, no! He's expecting us!" squealed Julie.

"Expecting you?" The first beast's expression grew suddenly fearful. "Do you mean to say that you four are the terrible . . . Blugs?"

"Blugs?" said Neal. "Sure. That's us!"

"Then Emperor Ko wants to see you right away!" said the first guard. "He must be informed that you are here." He lifted a small horn and blew into it. *Wooo!* "Come with us now —"

"Wait!" boomed a voice from inside the chamber. "Send them in . . . for a moment."

Trembling, the two beasts bowed. "Yes, Lord Gethwing. Of course, Lord Gethwing!"

The guards parted to let the four friends into the moon dragon's chamber. When they entered, they found Gethwing next to a large, flaming cauldron, sprinkling something into it. Sparr was standing nearby, his face turned to the ground.

Eric wanted to speak silently to him but dared not, in case Gethwing overheard.

But the moment Sparr raised his head and saw his friends, his eyes widened.

He knows us! thought Eric.

Gethwing turned. "So, you are the famous Blugs, are you? Emperor Ko has asked for you, but I wanted to see you first."

The moon dragon paced slowly in front of the fiery cauldron. Then he spoke in a low voice, almost a whisper. "Find me when you are done with Ko. I have a mission for you. A special mission."

What's this all about? wondered Eric.

"Emperor Ko wishes to restore the Empire of Goll," Gethwing continued. "But there are some who do not want to look to the past. They are looking to the future. Do you understand?"

Eric glanced meaningfully at Keeah. He knew what Gethwing meant. Sparr had been telling the kids for a long time that the dragon was looking for beasts to join him against Ko. He wanted to rule the beasts himself.

"You want a new Goll," squeaked Eric.

With a horrible twist of his jaws, Gethwing smiled icily at the disguised children. "I see we understand one another. After all, I can offer you many things. Look into the flames!"

He tossed more dust into the fire, and visions began to take shape in the smoke. There were mountains of gold and jewels, great wheeled chariots, and armies of wing-snakes, poised and ready for flight.

"A new Goll shall rise from the ashes of

the old!" cried the moon dragon. "And it can be yours, if you join me. Today's battle will —"

"Lord Gethwing!" came a sudden call from outside. "The fleet is ready to sail! Ko has demanded that you inspect the ships!"

The dragon waved his hand, and the visions vanished. Gazing coldly at the children, he said, "Say nothing of what you have seen! Sparr, take them to Ko!"

Gethwing then turned and stalked out of the chamber with his guards.

Sparr waited another moment, then exhaled as if he had been holding his breath for hours. "You guys! I'm so glad to see you! But why did you say you're the Blugs?"

"It was either that or be captured," said Keeah.

"It doesn't matter, anyway," said Eric. "We needed to get in here to get you out."

Sparr's expression was halfway between

a smile and a frown. "Thanks, but it won't be that easy. No one's ever seen the Blugs, not even Ko. They operate in secret. So that's good. But now that everyone knows you're here, you'll have to see him. Otherwise, he'll turn this whole place over looking for you —" He stopped. "Wait. Is Kem . . . nearby?"

Julie nodded. "With Galen and Shago."

"I sense him," said Sparr.

"But what's so important about the Blugs?" asked Keeah.

Sparr went to the mouth of the chamber and looked down on the sea below. "The Blugs are all about secret missions. Ko sent them on one, and now he wants to know things. I hope you don't actually know the information that he wants, because he'll use the Coiled Viper to force it out of you."

The Coiled Viper was a crown of great power. It was the Viper that had transformed Sparr into a boy when he used it to wake Emperor Ko from his age-old sleep.

Eric stood next to Sparr at the opening. "What do you know about this Shadowface guy? Have you seen him? Why is he helping Ko?"

"We even thought he cursed us," said Julie. "He said a weird word. *Nyora*. But nothing happened. Who is he?"

Just then, a terrible shout came from the shore below. "Bring the Blugs! Now!"

"Too late," said Sparr. "We have to go —"

But before they could move — *whoomf!* — purple flames leaped up from the cauldron. An image rose out of the smoke. But it wasn't like the visions that Gethwing conjured. It was the form of a cloaked figure.

"That's him!" said Julie. "Shadowface!"

Sparr gaped at the fire, and he began to quiver. The creature's burning red eyes seemed to penetrate the boy's. Then the rasping and whispering began.

"He's going to speak again!" said Keeah.

"*Nyora . . . peskah . . .*" the creature said.

Eric braced himself for something else. But as before, nothing happened. Shadowface disappeared into nothing.

Sparr pulled away from the cauldron and stood wobbling on his feet. He rubbed his eyes over and over as if they hurt from being too close to the fire. "Who *is* that? And what are those words? I don't know what they mean! Why is he here? What does he want?"

Eric thought that Sparr looked as helpless as he had ever seen him. "We don't know yet. But we need you. Galen said there won't be peace in Droon if you're not part of it. We have to get you out of here. We have to stick together to get through this."

"We all feel that way," said Keeah.

"It's called teamwork," said Neal.

The boy stopped rubbing his eyes and looked at the children for a long time. Finally, he managed a little smile. "Sometimes I can't believe I have any friends. For hundreds of years, I've been so totally alone. Now, for the first time, you guys . . ."

He turned away. "Anyway, let's not get all mushy. We have work to do. Ko will be angry if we take too long. Believe me, I know."

Sparr led them out of the chamber and began the steep climb down the stone face. Watching him move along the paths to the shore, Eric paused. He had the feeling that even though they were all together, Sparr was really in a place all by himself.

"Eric, come on," called Sparr. "Team-work, remember?"

"Coming," he said, hurrying one foot after another after another down to the black shore behind his friend.

Five

The Pirate King

When they arrived at the water's edge, the children were stunned by the massive size of the Skorth ships.

Altogether, nine black-planked vessels, eerie and frightening, had been raised. Their sails were ripped and sagging, their hulls shabby and crooked, but they bobbed in the water ready to sail into battle all the same. At the helm of each was a single

Skorth warrior, dripping wet, draped with strings of seaweed.

"Where are Galen, Shago, and Kem?" whispered Julie. "We could sure use them now."

Eric's heart sank as he scanned the shore, trying to spot their three friends. "What could they do against a navy like this, anyway?"

Gethwing silently trod along the northern bank of the channel, inspecting the ships.

All at once, the call came — "Bring the Blugs to Emperor Ko!" — and a pair of dark-scaled lizards tramped along the shore toward the children.

Sparr shook his head. "From Gethwing's fiery pot into Ko's fire. Sorry, guys."

The lizards hissed, turned, and ushered them down to the emperor's ship, a terrifying vessel nearly twice the size of the others. Beasts of all shapes and sizes, including large bearlike creatures and spiky gray lions, were tugging the ghostly rigging into position. They hoisted moldy sails up the crooked mast. They loaded rusty cannons with gnarled chunks of iron.

On the rear deck, dressed in jet-black robes and seated like a pirate king, was the bull-headed beast ruler, Ko. The crown called the Coiled Viper sat low on his brow, its twin snake heads gleaming in the light of the torches ranged along the deck. But as bright as the crown was, Ko's three red eyes blazed with an even stronger flame.

"Come forward, Blugs!" Ko boomed when he saw the children. He stared at them one by one with his terrifying eyes. Then he spoke.

"I do not know you. But when I was told that the Blugs possessed a certain talent, I commanded that you perform a single mission for the glory of Ko."

The emperor rose from his seat. Towering over the children, he scanned their beastly disguises. "You see we are ready to sail. Tell me now! What have you learned?"

Eric began to tremble. *What were the Blugs supposed to do for Ko?* He wondered if anyone could see his shaggy fur quivering.

"Why are you silent?" roared the emperor. "I commanded you to sneak into Jaffa City and find its weakest point. My ships are ready. Where shall we attack?"

He glared at the four children. All of a sudden, a blue glow from the Coiled Viper fell over Keeah.

"Ah!" Ko roared. "The crown tells me that *you* know the answer. Tell me now!"

Bathed in the light from the emperor's

magic crown, Keeah took a wobbly step forward. "The . . . sea . . ." she said.

Sparr moved close behind her. *Careful, Keeah. Don't look at the Viper!*

But the princess took another step, as if drawn forward into the magic light.

"The seawall . . ." she said, seeming to struggle against the power of the Coiled Viper, but failing. "The seawall to the west. It's the oldest in the city. And . . . the weakest!"

"Well done, my spies! Sparr, take them below!" said Ko. He quickly turned to the Skorth warrior at the wheel. The moment he did, the light of the Viper subsided, and Keeah came out of her trance.

"What just happened?" she whispered. "What did I do? Oh, no. My Jaffa City!"

"We sail now!" bellowed Ko. "There is no stopping us! Skorth, take us to Jaffa City's western seawall!"

All at once, the skeleton warriors on all the ships spun their great wooden wheels.

The torn sails filled magically with the black air of the Dark Lands. One after the other, the ships moved over the waves toward the Horns of Ko.

Then, suddenly, everything happened at once.

No sooner had the ships begun to move across the waves than a call came from the shore. "The Blugs have arrived!"

The children whirled around and saw four furry beasts standing on the shore, shouting up at the ship. "Hey! Who are them beasts?"

"Uh-oh!" gasped Neal.

But before the emperor could react, a strange rumbling sounded and a dense purple fog drifted over the deck, obscuring everything.

"Shadowface is back!" said Eric.

From the fog, the children heard three words.

"*Nyora! Peskah! Toth!*"

"Yeah, yeah," mumbled Neal. "It still means nothing —"

All of a sudden, Sparr fell to his knees and clamped his hands over his ears, his face twisted in pain. Then he began shouting, "*Nyora. Peskah. Toth. Nyora — peskah — toth. Toth! Toth!*"

Screaming loudly, Sparr flew across the deck straight at Emperor Ko, his fingers blasting red sparks. *Blam-blam-blam!* Lightning sliced across the deck. Before the beasts could protect their ruler, Sparr leaped at him. He yanked the Coiled Viper from Ko's forehead.

"What! Nooooo —" roared Ko.

Jumping away, Sparr blasted the emperor with his free hand. Ko toppled backward into a band of beasts and fell over the railing and into the water. *Splash!*

"Holy cow!" gasped Eric.

Sparr turned on the rest of the crew next, blasting them off the deck and into the black waves one by one, leaving only the Skorth captain at the helm. Finally, he stepped toward the children. His eyes glassy, his face blank, he fired blast upon blast at their feet and sent them all flying overboard after Ko.

Even before the children struck the icy water, the Skorth captain spun the ghostly wheel and turned the ship on the waves, crashing this way and that through the fleet.

"Sparr!" Eric yelled, shivering in the waves. "Stop! What are you doing?"

Sparr turned, his fins as black as night, his eyes red with rage. Seeming to struggle against the purple fog that wrapped around him, he spoke silently to Eric.

It's Shadowface. He's calling me!

The boy wrenched himself away as the emperor's giant vessel plowed violently past the last ship and into the open waters of the ink-dark Serpent Sea.

"Sparr!" cried Ko, storming to the shore. "Stop the boy! Stop him —"

Then came a terrible call from the lookout at the top of the Horns of Ko.

"King Zello's navy is approaching! Prepare to open the Horns! We are at war!"

Six

The Ink-Dark Sea

Icy waves sloshed wildly over the children, but they managed to swim to the bank just as Ko roared a command.

"Beasts, we shall follow Sparr later! Prepare to open the Horns! Bring me a ship!"

"Let's lose the beast disguises," said Eric, breathlessly climbing onshore. "We need our powers back."

"To help my father's fleet!" said Keeah. "Hurry!"

Unrolling his scroll and shaking it as dry as he could, Neal reversed the charm with Julie's help, and the kids were themselves again. But Ko was already at the helm of a second Skorth vessel, piloting his navy toward the Horns.

"We need to get up to the top of the Horns right now," said Julie. "Let's fly. Neal?"

"All aboard!" he said.

Taking their friends' hands, Neal and Julie flew them all quickly and unseen to the top of the giant stone heads. From there, they could clearly see the approaching royal fleet.

"Everyone's there on the *Jaffa Wind*," said Keeah. "My parents and Max, too."

They saw the spider troll working the great wooden wheel on the upper deck of the ship. Keeah's father stood tall at the prow, looking through a long, golden spyglass, while her mother stood by his side, clutching a big blue book.

"She must have discovered something in Agrah-Voor's library," said Eric. "Something about Shadowface."

There was a sudden flash of black and the flap of heavy wings in the distant sky. It was Gethwing. He dived toward the sea, circled once, then soared up again.

Almost instantly, the water began to bubble and churn off the left side of the royal fleet.

Zello yelled something to Max. The great vessel turned, and the Droon navy followed its lead.

"Our ships are going to battle the serpents," said Keeah, her voice quivering. Eric's eyes widened as he realized she was right.

At the same time, the Skorth ships jostled inside the closed gates, eager to burst out onto the open seas and attack the distracted navy. Several jagged-finned serpents had already begun to batter the king's ships.

Ko bellowed, "Open the Horns! Open them! We attack now!"

Errrch! With a deep wrenching sound, the scraping of stone on stone, and a violent sloshing of waves, the enormous rocks of the Horns of Ko began to part.

"Noooo!" yelled Keeah. "The Skorth will ambush our navy while they're battling the serpents. We have to help them — oh!"

Blam! A burst of violet sparks accidentally escaped from her fingertips, loosening some rocks at her feet. They skittered down the side of the stone head and landed on the deck of Ko's ship with a loud crash.

The emperor looked up, scanning his own giant likeness.

"Uh-oh," said Julie. "He'll see us —"

"No, that's it!" cried Keeah suddenly. "Let's blast the ground and start a rock slide — right onto those creepy ships. We can delay their attack on the navy! Eric —"

At once, the two wizards sent bolt after bolt of sparks at the ground beneath their feet.

Blam! Blam! Loose rocks tumbled down the face of the stone head and smashed onto the decks of the Skorth vessels crowded below.

The beasts aimed their cannons at the top of the heads and fired. But the cannon blasts only sent more rocks toppling down at them.

"Stop firing, you fools!" Ko shouted. "Pull away from the cliffs!"

The ships began to retreat from the Horns, slamming into one another in their haste to clear the falling rocks.

"Traffic jam!" said Neal. "That's what we like to see!"

Meanwhile, cannons shot from Zello's ships at the sea creatures. Relna blasted the waves with a thin stream of blue sparks.

"Now, Eric," yelled Keeah. "Let's blast the water. Make it too hot for the serpents!"

"You got it!" said Eric. "One, two, three —"

Whoom! Blam! Both wizards sent powerful bolts at the sea from their position atop the Horns. Squealing and shrieking, the attacking sea serpents dived away to the cooler depths, leaving Zello's royal navy free to sail straight to the open Horns.

"Yahoo!" cried Julie. "Teamwork does it again!"

"Close the Horns!" sputtered Ko, and the channel filled with the sound of iron wheels turning and stones coming together. "Draw back from the gates —"

"That's not so easy when you reverse the steering!" boomed a familiar voice.

The kids turned to see Galen racing along the top of the stone head, his curved staff blazing with light. He was completely soaked.

"Galen!" said Keeah. "Where have you been?"

"Sabotaging the ships!" chirped Shago, who scampered up behind the wizard, with Kem, both shaking themselves dry. "Now, everyone, watch this —"

Crash! Plonk! Crunchhhh!

As the Skorth ships drew away from the Horns, they began sailing in circles, crashing into one another.

Seeing his chance, Zello gave out a loud whoop, and Max piloted the *Jaffa Wind* neatly between the Horns of Ko. *Booom!* It rammed right into the emperor's floundering ship.

"Now, back to the shore and into the ship!" said Galen. No sooner had Neal and Julie flown the little group back down than Max steered the *Jaffa Wind* right to them.

"Come aboard, everyone!" said the queen as a landing plank splashed to the shore. "We have a Sparr to catch!"

As the seven friends raced onto the ship, a dozen small sails shot up, and a pair of massive steam engines groaned to life.

"Speed ahead, Max!" Keeah urged. "With everything we have."

"And we have a lot!" said Max.

Whoomf-whoomf! White steam shot up from the smokestacks in the stern. With a roar and a shout from its crew, the *Jaffa Wind* crashed through the enemy fleet. It sped after Sparr's vessel, now nearly out of sight on the icy black water of the Serpent Sea.

Seven

Snake Island . . . Again

A storm was rising over the black sea. Wind blew in widening circles, churning the waves. One second, the sea surged and launched the *Jaffa Wind* high. The next second, great hollows of water pulled the hull back down with an angry *thud*.

"Faster now! Hoist every sail, use all steam power, and . . . forward!" cried Zello.

Galen stood next to the king, rain lashing his face, the light of his rainbow staff piercing the gloom. "Eric, Keeah, everyone, come here, please," he said.

The two wizards scrambled across the deck and joined their friends.

"We had some fun at the Horns of Ko," said Galen. "But our journey now is a dark one. Relna, please tell us what you know."

The queen opened the large blue book the children had seen earlier.

"Hazad and I found something," she said. "Something, but not everything. The language you heard is more of a mystery than ever."

"What can you tell us?" asked Shago.

"*'Nyora peskah toth'* is a phrase in a secret language unlike all other Droon languages," Relna said. "As you have noticed, the first two words mean little until the final word is uttered. The last word acts like a key, unlocking the meaning — and the power — of all the words before it."

"But what do the words mean?" asked Keeah.

Relna breathed deeply. "It is a command. As near as we can tell, it means 'steal the crown.' The words are from a language as old as Droon, but one that died out completely when the Goll empire rose to power. According to the elders of Agrah-Voor, however, the language was revived by Lord Sparr and used by him alone to cloak his own darkest magic."

"By him alone?" said Eric, peering out at the black sea. "But that's impossible. That hooded sorcerer knows it, too."

Shago made a noise. "And we still don't know who this mysterious Shadowboots is!"

Neal opened his mouth, then shook his head. "No. I'm not going to say it."

"We may not know *who* he is," said Max, studying the charts spread out on the deck next to him, "but we do know *where* he is. From this chart I can tell where he's taking Sparr . . . and *us*. . . ." Clinging to the wheel, the spider troll pointed to a strangely shaped island on his map. "There."

Galen looked from the map out to the far-off sea. He groaned under his breath.

"There, indeed," he grumbled. "There . . . again!"

In the distant sea off the port bow stood a stone island with the likeness of a head.

It was the head of a giant snake, ready to pounce.

"Kahfoo Mountain?" gasped Keeah.

"Just so," snarled King Zello.

Kahfoo was the primeval snake that Sparr had befriended long ago. The snake itself was no more, but its island home remained in the very center of the Serpent Sea.

Neal grumbled, "Did you ever notice how bad guys like making giant models of their heads around here? I mean, haven't they ever heard of taking pictures?"

"Look," said Julie, pointing to the wisps of purple fog drifting around the island. "As if we needed any proof, Shadowface is definitely there."

"Steady now," said Zello as they pulled closer. "Lower the sails. Cut the power!"

Max shut off the steam engines, and everything went quiet except for the lapping of waves against the wooden hull.

Drifting around the coast, they saw the back of Sparr's ghostly ship disappearing into a high, arched cavern beneath the island.

"An underground grotto," said Galen. He held his staff tightly. "We must follow him in. Hurry now. With every moment, Sparr is in more danger."

"I'm afraid for him," said Relna. "He's under this creature's control."

Right, thought Eric. *I hope we can get to him in time!*

Within minutes, the *Jaffa Wind* slipped inside the grotto. Stealthily, the ship followed the purple fog under the island, worming its way between the cave's jagged walls.

Galen's eyes strained to pierce the gloom ahead. "Whoever Shadowface is, he possesses a dark will, darker perhaps than any I have known."

Waving away the drifting purple fog, Eric couldn't get Sparr's last look out of his mind. It was hopeless, angry, and frightened all at once. "Hurry," was all he could say. "Hurry."

There was the sudden sound of a wooden hull thudding against stones. Then came the hesitant patter of footsteps.

Kem whimpered and pointed.

"There!" whispered Keeah, following the dog's gaze.

On the far side of the channel, they saw the Skorth ship docked and unmoving. The black-cloaked boy was running up a set of stairs hewn from the rock, then pausing as if drawn against his will.

"Sparr!" called Zello. "Sparr, wait! You need us with you —"

"I doubt he can hear us anymore," said Galen. "His mind hears only the words of Shadowface's commands now. Come!"

Leaping down onto the bank before their ship had even docked, the group of friends ran straight to the steps. But the moment they began to climb, three massively armed Skorth warriors appeared at the opening at the top of the stairs. Their jaws hung open, and they seemed to be grinning.

"More bone boys?" murmured Neal. "I thought there were only nine."

"Unless Shadowface has conjured more of them," said Max.

Clack — click — clack! The warriors began to descend the steps.

Relna's hands were already sparking. "Children, Galen, follow Sparr. The king and I will handle this."

"We'll keep them busy!" said Zello, unslinging his giant club and twirling it in his hand. "Come on, smiley boys, wipe those grins off your faces!"

As Relna crouched and sent a blast of blue sparks into the midst of the Skorth, Zello rushed right at the warriors, whacking any who managed to make it past the queen.

No sooner had the Skorth fallen to pieces than they began to reassemble themselves.

"That's my arm!" growled one bone creature. "Here's your foot!"

And as quickly as they came together again, the teamwork of the king and queen blasted them apart.

"Keep them busy, indeed!" said Galen with a chuckle. "There's old-fashioned Droon bravery! Come, children, Kem. Up the steps. Now!"

As the battle continued, the eight companions jumped through the black opening and into a winding passage. Following it, they felt themselves moving up toward the center of the island. The air was heavy, clammy, and hard to breathe. Every now and then, they could hear a familiar humming sound echoing off the walls of the passage.

"Hurry! Time is running short!" urged Max.

They charged ahead faster, slowing

finally before an opening in the passage. A faint purple light flickered deep within.

"So," Galen whispered. "Here we are, in the presence of great evil. Let's enter together. Side by side, if it helps."

"Oh, it does," said Julie, shivering.

One, two, three silent steps, and the group of friends was inside the eerie chamber. Tall columns supported a ceiling in which two red stones, the eyes of the stone snake head, stood fixed and glowing.

The little band slid into the shadows and remained still, barely breathing.

Crouched on the floor in the center of the room lay the dark heap of a boy — Sparr. He did not move. Nothing did. It seemed to the children as if time had stopped dead inside the awful chamber.

Kem whimpered softly, but Neal hushed him, holding him back.

Eric whispered, "Sparr?"

But no sooner had the name left his lips than a coil of purple mist appeared among the shadows and began to take shape.

Eight

The Storm Rises

As the purple fog whirled before their eyes, Galen spoke silently, *Max, Shago —* *follow me. Children, keep hidden. Watch* *for my signal.*

The wizard, the spider troll, and the thief slid to the left of the opening and moved silently away, while Keeah, Julie, Neal, Kem, and Eric darted to the right.

Moments later, Shadowface seemed to

materialize out of the purple fog. He stood looming over the boy, a hazy, frightening form of swirling smoke and tattered rags.

"S . . . S . . . Sparr . . ." he whispered from under his hood. "You un . . . understood my c-c-command, didn't you, boy?"

Sparr moved on the floor, then went still.

"What a memory is locked in th-that young head of yours! *Nyora peskah . . . toth*. You recalled the words as only you c-c-could —"

The old man wheezed. The sound of his swallowing was like marbles tumbling down a long drain.

Sparr, we're here, said Eric silently, spying the others hiding in place behind Shadowface. *We'll help you. Make a sign if you can hear me. . . .*

The boy raised his head slightly but did not turn toward Eric.

"Give me the V-V-Viper," Shadowface commanded.

When Sparr lifted the golden crown, the man's arm rose to receive it. As it did, his sleeve slid back, revealing a pale hand, thin and bloodless.

Eric felt his own hands warming, his fingertips ready to spark.

In one swift move, Shadowface snatched the Viper away from Sparr. Immediately, the boy seemed released from his trance.

"Shadowface!" he snarled, shaking his head as if to clear it. "What just happened? How did you make me steal the Viper? How *could* you? And how do you know that language? I'm the only one alive who knows it. Who *are* you?"

In the near silence that followed, Eric heard that strange humming once more.

Whatever was making the sound was moving closer.

Shadowface didn't answer Sparr, but as he stared at the boy, the purple fog around him grew darker and denser.

Sparr staggered, clutching his chest.

"What's wrong with me?" he asked, panicked.

"Ooh, ooh, I know!" said Shadowface, his voice growing deeper, less breathy. "And so do you. Remember the Isle of Mists? You suffered a transformation there. A change. You became young. But such was the power of this Viper that something else happened, too. Some*one* else happened. . . ."

Keeah gasped. *Eric, what does he mean*?

"Part of Lord Sparr was thrown back to his childhood. . . ." Shadowface said, raising his white hand and moving it up toward his head.

Part of him? said Keeah silently.

"That part of him," said Shadowface, "became a boy. That part of him became *you. . . .*"

"What are you talking about?" said Sparr, breathing hard. "It's not true —"

"The other part of the dark lord," Shadowface continued, "was thrown ahead to the end of his life. Instead of being young and fresh and bright like you, he woke up old, withered, used up, at the very edge of death."

"No! I don't believe it!" said Sparr.

"You never knew you were half a person, did you, boy?" Shadowface snarled.

Sparr tried to speak, but Eric heard only the boy's breathing. It was labored and shallow.

"While you joined with your new friends to battle Ko and Gethwing," said Shadowface, "the old half of you scuttled away from the Isle of Mists like a crab. He fed on the darkness, hoping to restore himself to who he once was. He has been waiting, boy, for the right time. That time has come."

As the figure paused to take a long, deep breath, Galen spoke silently. *Ready yourselves!*

"Who *are* you?" asked Sparr fearfully.

"Come now, boy. You've known me your whole life!"

Shadowface's pale hands slowly reached up, one on either side of his face, and began to pull the hood back.

Eric felt his blood turn to ice. His heart thundered in his chest.

"I . . ." Shadowface began.

The hood snagged for a second before sliding back.

"I am . . ."

He paused as the hood revealed first

one, then a second withered black fin sticking up from behind his ears.

"I am . . . you!"

Sparr quaked suddenly, then slumped to the ground. "No, no, no!"

Removing his hood completely now, Shadowface looked as Sparr himself might have looked if he were centuries old. The fins behind his ears were ancient and torn, ragged and lifeless. His skin was pale, almost see-through, and wrinkled beyond belief.

Eric's head throbbed.

Could this possibly be true? Is Shadowface really the other half of Sparr? Even in a magical place like Droon, is that even . . . possible?

"There was someone else on the Isle of Mists, wasn't there?" Shadowface continued. "Someone else who was split in two."

He turned slightly and gave out a low, broken whistle.

There came a tired growl, then an old beast loped slowly out of the shadows. A beast with two heads.

Oh, my gosh! thought Eric.

Sparr gasped. "Kem? Kem!"

It was Kem. Or rather it was Kem as he would look if he were hundreds of years old. His twin heads drooped, his hide sagged. One of his heads stared glassily to one side, while the other lifted itself painfully, tentatively to watch what was happening in the room.

From the moment the old dog appeared, Neal had kept his hands over the puppy's mouths to keep him silent. "Shhh, boy, shhh."

Spotting the boy on the floor, the old dog limped over on three legs, dragging the fourth to the side, and drooling all the way. He sniffed Young Sparr, then slumped on the floor next to him.

"Knowing that Ko was about to begin his final assault on free Droon," said the man, "I used what power I had to steal the Skorth bones. If I could help Ko with his battle, I could bring Droon to its darkest moment. This island is where the Empire of Goll began ten centuries ago. Here is where evil is at its most terrible. Here is where I can unite the two parts of myself again —"

"But I'm *not* part of you!" shouted Sparr. "I'm not . . . I can't be!"

"Oh, but I did it for you!" Shadowface pleaded in a mocking tone. "I led you here so you and I could become *ourself* again. Lord Sparr!"

"No —"

The sound of explosions and yelling

came from outside the mountain. The friends exchanged glances in the shadows.

The battle is just outside, thought Eric. *But there's an even bigger battle in here.*

"I have assembled an unbeatable force," said Shadowface. "More Skorth than anyone could ever imagine. They shall be my army! Ko and Gethwing will fight each other soon. One will lose, and the winner will fall to me. Only one person stands in my way now. Or rather, he crouches in my way. . . ."

"You're cracked," groaned Sparr.

"In two!" said the man with an icy laugh. "But we'll end that right now! What broke us apart will put us back together again —"

With that, Shadowface raised the Coiled Viper over his head. Beams of brilliant blue light engulfed the boy.

"No!" cried Sparr, frozen in the fierce light.

"No is right!" cried Galen at last, leaping from the shadows. "Sorcerer, you shall not win! Everyone, now!"

At once, the three wizards charged Shadowface, their blasts blazing, while Neal conjured a net of chains that he threw over the man. But Shadowface was ready for them. Sidestepping Neal's net, he threw a lightning bolt of red flame at Galen, knocking him, Shago, and Max across the room into Eric, Julie, and Keeah. Breaking free, Kem leaped over to Sparr and the old dog.

"Ha-ha! Already my strength begins to return!" Shadowface laughed.

"Blast him again!" cried Keeah. She, Eric, and Galen scrambled to their feet and sent a barrage of lightning bolts at Shadowface with all their might. But one after another, he parried them as more explosions burst outside. They were followed by the sound of wood splintering and of men and beasts falling and splashing into the Serpent Sea.

"Skorth!" shouted Shadowface. "Keep them from us — until *we* become . . . *me*!"

Whoomp! A burst of purple fog filled the room.

"My eyes!" cried Julie. "It stings!"

"And stinks!" added Neal, pinching his nose.

Keeah blew out a charmed breath and cleared the chamber. But Shadowface had vanished. So had Sparr. So had both Kems, young and old. In their place were row upon row of Skorth warriors. They were all grinning and all armed.

"Uh-oh," whispered Max. "I think we've stayed too long."

Nodding their skulls in agreement, the bone warriors charged.

Nine

Smiles of the Skorth

"Behind me, children!" shouted Galen, raising his shimmering staff. "You men of bone and iron were made from dark things. And to dark things you shall return — now!"

Galen swung his staff and knocked two bone warriors to the ground. Their pieces clattered across the floor, but they instantly began to reassemble themselves.

"Attack!" cried Shago.

Together, the seven friends launched themselves into the rows of Skorth warriors. They battled them out of the chamber, down the passages, up the stairs, out of every tunnel, and through one hall after another.

Up and down, right and left, backward and forward, the band of seven fought the fearful warriors, and slowly but surely coiled up farther inside the monstrous snake's stone head.

All the while, the sounds of the surrounding sea battle grew louder.

With a great triple blast from Keeah, Galen, and Eric, the friends managed to blow the Skorth into a pile of loose bones, trapping them in a narrow tunnel.

Neal searched his scroll furiously, then stopped with a grin. "We can't hurt them, but we can stop them!" With a quick murmur of words, he surrounded the bones in an enormous block of ice, sealing them in the tunnel.

"Skorth on ice," he said. "I like it!"

"Now — to Sparr!" said Eric. "Hurry!"

Following Galen's lead, they bolted up to the island's summit.

Bursting out the top of the snake's head, they saw Shadowface standing across from Sparr. The two dogs faced each other next to them. The sorcerer held one hand menacingly over the boy, while the other held the Coiled Viper. Its blue light enveloped Sparr like a cloud.

"We don't care who you are, Shadowcreep," shouted Neal. "Guys — blast him!"

Instinctively, the wizards sent a spray of multicolored sparks at the tall sorcerer.

Shadowface only laughed. For when the combined blasts struck, they seemed to have no effect on him, while young

Sparr crumpled to his knees and howled in pain.

"It isn't working!" said Keeah. "Eric, Galen, again —"

BLAM! BLAM! BLAM! The air over the island blazed with blue, violet, and silver light.

But with every blast, Shadowface seemed to grow more defined and real, while the boy faded.

"Stop! Stop!" cried the boy finally, writhing on the ground, trapped in the Viper's blue glow. "Don't you see? It's *me* you're attacking! He wants you to hurt me! He wants me to fade away to nothing! I'll be no more and he'll be young again —"

The old man laughed a chilling laugh. "He's right, you know! Care to fire again?"

As the Viper's light continued to fall over Sparr, the boy's cloak began to change from pitch-black to dark gray. At the same time, the old sorcerer's skin took on more color. Blood rose in his cheeks. He became younger and began to fire back at the children.

Ka-blam! Fooom!

Eric staggered back from the summit with his friends, taking shelter behind a mound of stone.

"Guys, what are we going to do . . . ?"

He stopped. No sooner had he asked his question than Eric knew what they had to do. He lowered his sparking hands.

"Eric —" said Keeah.

"We have to stop," he said. "The more we fire at Shadowface, the more we hurt Sparr."

"But he's draining our friend away to nothing!" cried Max. "I can't watch. He's evil, pure evil!"

The old sorcerer's attack on them did not cease. *Wha-boom! Blam!* Bolt after bolt of red flame exploded on their hiding place, while young Sparr grew still more blurry and lifeless. Kem, too, underwent the same change. His younger self lay weak and trembling next to the boy, while the old beast grew more hearty and youthful.

Even as anger rose in him, Eric felt his throat begin to sting. He turned to the wizard. "Galen, if we let them join together, could there, I mean, could there still be some of our friend in him? Could he . . . survive?"

Galen watched his little brother helplessly. Heaving a deep sigh, he said, "Perhaps it's not our hatred for Shadowface but our love for Sparr that may save even a small part of him. My mother hoped it would be so. Maybe it's our only hope, too —"

Boom! Splash! The battle on the Serpent Sea raged all around the island now. The Skorth vessels sank ship after ship of the royal fleet, while Relna sent charms from the shore and brought the Droon ships bobbing quickly to the surface again.

"But unless we stop Shadowface, Sparr won't survive!" cried Julie.

"He may," said Galen as the sorcerer's blasts continued to explode over them. "He may. But only as part of the greater sorcerer. I fear the time of young Sparr is ending. Evil must win. At least for now."

Galen lowered his sparkling staff.

Keeah let her hands fall to her sides.

Their attack on Shadowface ended.

Seeing this, the sorcerer's skin flushed with new life, and he began to laugh.

Ten

From Hand to Hand to Hand

Second by second, the Viper did its work, and young Sparr faded. His older self, towering over the quivering heap, became younger. He was nearly as young as he had been on the Isle of Mists.

The sorcerer snapped his fingers, and no fewer than fifty Skorth warriors emerged from the depths of the island. They took their place in front of him.

"I can't stand it!" said Eric, his chest

heaving. He turned to Galen. "Isn't there anything we can do to help our friend? Anything at all?"

Galen looked at his younger brother and closed his eyes briefly. When he did, Eric thought the wizard looked as old as he ever had. And he knew why. He was losing his brother to evil once again.

Galen reached out and took Eric's hand, wrapping his own fingers firmly around it. "Perhaps there is one hope," he said. "One hope . . . if you . . ."

"Yes." Eric pulled his hand away from Galen and turned to Sparr. Even in the few seconds he hadn't been watching, the boy had become nearly invisible.

Grasping Galen's staff, he hurled himself over the ridge of stone right at the Skorth warriors, swinging in a blur of colored light.

Flang! Crack! Whump! Plong!

Skulls fell, bones toppled as the warriors whirled away from him. All the while, the sorcerer, cackling more loudly by the minute, grew into himself again. The purple fog was nearly gone now. His black cloak shimmered in the blue light showering from the Viper.

With one final swing, Eric pushed the last warrior behind him and knelt next to the boy and to the small dog that lay still beside him. Galen's staff deflected the Viper's light from Eric, but not from Sparr. It cast its glow through him to the ground below.

"Sparr . . ." he whispered.

The boy shook his head. "Save yourselves. I'm going pretty quickly now. . . ."

Sparr's skin was almost translucent, his cloak as white and thin as gauze.

"You can't go, you can't leave us," Eric said, barely able to get the words out. "All this time we needed you . . . we *still* need you! You're . . . good. . . ."

"Yeah, well," the boy faltered, "all good things . . . must end. . . ." He coughed and seemed to begin sinking into the ground itself, as the last bit of color that remained in him bled away.

Eric took Sparr's pale hand and pressed his own firmly around it, as if he never wanted to let go. "I hope . . ." he started to say, his eyes welling with tears. "I hope . . . you'll . . ."

He couldn't go on.

"Eric, don't ever stop hoping," Sparr said feebly. He writhed in pain for a moment. Then he managed one last smile and said, "Hey, it's been fun."

With that, the Viper's glow penetrated the boy completely, settling over him like a shroud. Sparr grew whiter and blurrier, and

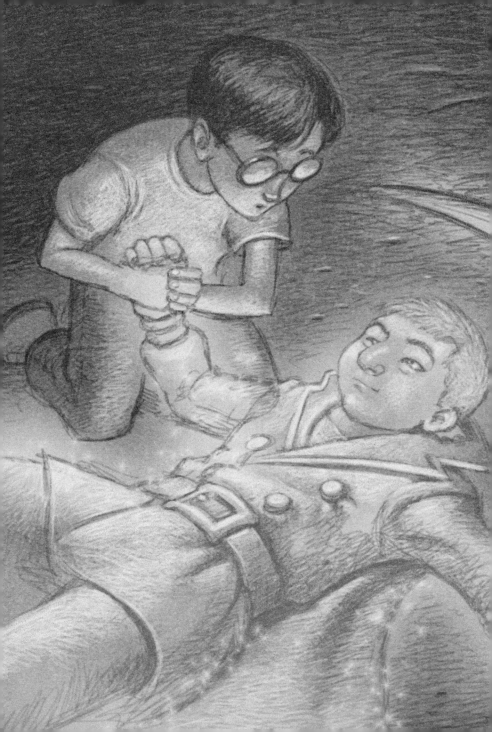

finally drifted away into the dark lord himself.

The Viper's brilliant light vanished.

Lord Sparr grinned. He had returned.

"Well, lookee here!" he said, flicking his jagged fins playfully. "I'm back!"

Eric stood and turned to the new Lord Sparr. He didn't know what to think or how to feel. The boy who had helped them for so long, the boy who had become their friend, was no more.

And the boy's older self had killed him.

Without knowing why, Eric took a step toward Lord Sparr. Trembling, almost crying, his heart exploding in his chest, he spoke.

"Why the Skorth?" he asked.

Lord Sparr glared down at him. "Eh, boy?"

"Why not the Ninns? I mean, they've been waiting for you to come back for ages.

There are thousands of them. They would follow you anywhere! Why are you using the Skorth warriors now?"

The eyes that he had known as a friend's for so long stared back at him now, fiery and dark.

"Because . . ." said Lord Sparr, turning away. "Because the Skorth have no souls."

At that moment, Ko's bellowing echoed up the side of the island to its summit.

Sparr grimaced. "It seems I have more enemies than just you today. Now you know why I had to steal the Viper. But I should go. I'll leave you to mourn the passing of . . . oh, wait . . . I'm not dead! Sorry we can't finish our little battle. But as someone once said — all good things must end. For now, anyway!"

Eric stared at Lord Sparr, searching for a sign that he understood what he had just said, but the sorcerer turned away too swiftly.

Suddenly, the rumbling that the children had been hearing all day grew to a deafening roar.

"What —" Keeah gasped.

A shape rose up in the air over the summit of the island. It was an enormous golden creature, with giant wings flapping so quickly they couldn't be seen.

"The Golden Wasp!" cried Galen. "Sparr has found him!"

Buzzing and spitting, the huge Wasp lowered to the ground next to Sparr. Holding the Coiled Viper tightly in his left hand, the sorcerer climbed up onto the Wasp's back. Kem, restored to healthy middle-age, leaped up next to his master. A moment later, the Wasp lifted from the island.

As it turned and swept away into the

dark sky, Eric spotted Sparr's right hand. Clutched in it was the small object that Galen had given to Eric and Eric had given to young Sparr.

It was the black stone that Sparr's mother had always wanted him to have.

The sorcerer's hand closed around it tightly, even as he laughed a cold, cruel laugh.

"Buh-bye, all!" he shouted.

In a flash, the Wasp soared up into the black clouds.

No sooner had Sparr gone than the fleet of ghostly ships began to sail after him. But now the decks were jammed with thousands of skeleton warriors, armored pirates, a vast multitude of the fearless Skorth.

At Emperor Ko's command, the beasts leaped from the vessels and into the churning Serpent Sea below.

Fuming and yelling from atop a

gargantuan finned serpent, and shaking his four fists at the sky, Ko now uttered a chilling curse.

"Beasts, everywhere, follow me! Sparr! Traitor! Liar! I shall hunt you down across the length and breadth of this world. Aye, across every other world, too! You shall never escape me! I will have the Coiled Viper again. I will have you — *Lord Sparr!*"

Bowing to the emperor's words, Gethwing swept after Sparr, too, a massive swarm of wingsnakes flying in formation behind him.

The Droon royal fleet docked at the island, and the fearful battle was over.

Gathering together on the summit of Kahfoo Mountain, the friends were quiet for a long time.

Finally, Julie spoke. "We lost . . . we lost a friend today," she said, faltering once, then again before she continued. "Sparr was our only hope. . . ."

"Perhaps he still is," said Galen, scanning the distant sea. "Droon is poised in a fearful balance. It may all depend on that little black stone. But time is not on our side —"

Whoosh! A shining light appeared over the children. The magical staircase had returned.

Keeah looked at her friends. "It's time for you to go. But if I know anything, I know that we'll soon be following Sparr."

"Deeper into the Dark Lands?" asked Neal.

"And beyond," said Galen, his eyes still fixed on the horizon. "If I am right, we'll see parts of Droon we've never seen before."

"Until then, we shall think and plan," said Max. "Hurry now, everyone. Quickly!"

Waving good-bye to their Droon friends, Eric, Neal, and Julie ran up the staircase.

Halfway up, they paused and looked down. The royal fleet was already heading back toward the Horns of Ko.

"What if our time with Sparr made no difference at all?" said Julie. "Looking at his face at the end, I'm not sure. Maybe there *is* no hope for Droon. What if it only gets worse?"

Neal hung his head, shaking it from side to side. "This is the worst. I feel empty. Sick. I don't care if I ever eat again."

Exhausted and sad beyond belief, Eric remembered over and over the image of young Sparr's hand weakly but lovingly closing over his mother's stone.

Don't ever stop hoping, Sparr had told him.

Eric couldn't help feeling that maybe there really *was* hope. But it existed in the unlikeliest of objects. And now that Lord Sparr was back, evil and powerful once more, that hope rested with the unlikeliest of people.

And still, he thought as he hurried home with his friends, *I hope . . . I hope . . . I hope*.

About the Author

Tony Abbott is the author of more than sixty funny novels for young readers, including the popular Danger Guys books and The Weird Zone series, as well as *Kringle*, his hardcover novel from Scholastic Press. Since childhood, he has been drawn to stories that challenge the imagination, and, like Eric, Julie, and Neal, he often dreamed of finding doors that open to other worlds. Now that he is older — though not quite as old as Galen Longbeard — he believes he may have found some of those doors. They are called books. Tony Abbott was born in Ohio and now lives with his wife and two daughters in Connecticut. For more information about Tony Abbott and the continuing saga of Droon, visit www.tonyabbottbooks.com.